DARKNESS SLIPPED IN

For my friends and family
and thanks to Steve, Mike and the AHRC

KINGFISHER

First published 2008 by Kingfisher
an imprint of Macmillan Children's Books
a division of Macmillan Publishers Limited
20 New Wharf Road, London N1 9RR
Basingstoke and Oxford
www.panmacmillan.com

Associated companies throughout the world

ISBN 978-0-7534-1531-3

Text and illustrations copyright © Ella Burfoot 2008

The right of Ella Burfoot to be identified as the
author of this work has been asserted by her in accordance
with the Copyright, Designs and Patents Act 1988.

1 3 5 7 9 8 6 4 2
1TR/0108/THOM/SCHOY(SCHOY)/157MA/C

A CIP catalogue record for this book is available from the British Library.

Printed in India

Darkness Slipped In

Ella Burfoot

KINGFISHER

Daisy was thinking of a game to play

when Darkness slipped in at the end of the day.

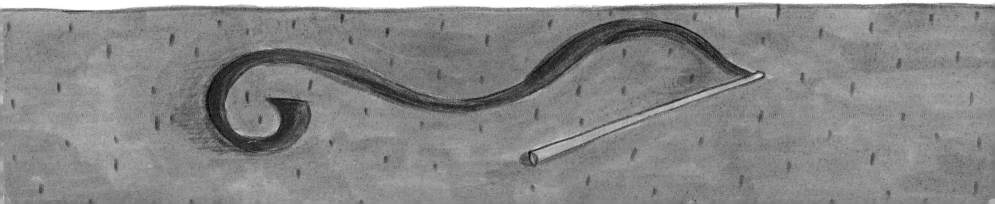

He came in through the window
and spread out on the floor.

While Daisy danced and laughed and played –
then danced around some more.

Pretending that he wasn't there,
he slid along the wall.

But Daisy had seen Darkness
and she wasn't scared at all.

Darkness quickly filled the room
and ate up all the light.

But Daisy knew
that Darkness knew

she had him in her sight.

With one swift move
she crossed the room
and grabbed him by the wrist.

And pretty soon,
around the room,

they danced the FUNKY TWIST!

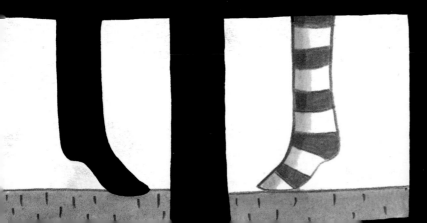

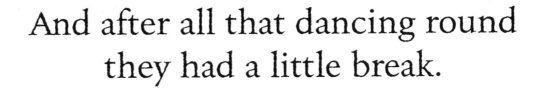

And after all that dancing round
they had a little break.

They sipped a cup of lemonade
and nibbled on some cake.

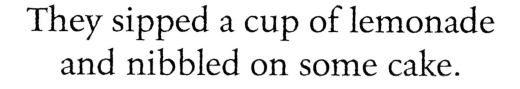

Now Darkness comes
in every night

to dance and laugh and play.

And the two of them, best of friends,
dance the night away.

But when they're tired and sleepy,
Daisy switches off the light.
And Daisy knows
that Darkness knows
it's time to say . . .

"Goodnight."